When...

Emma Dodd

templar publishing

When I grow up,
I want to be...

clever and funny,

wild and free.

When I grow up, I want to be...

big and strong,

and **tall** as a tree.

When I grow up, I want to go
all over the world,
in sun and snow.

When I grow up, I want to do...

kind things, loving things...

just like **you**.

When I grow up, I want to **be**
all the things that make me...

me!

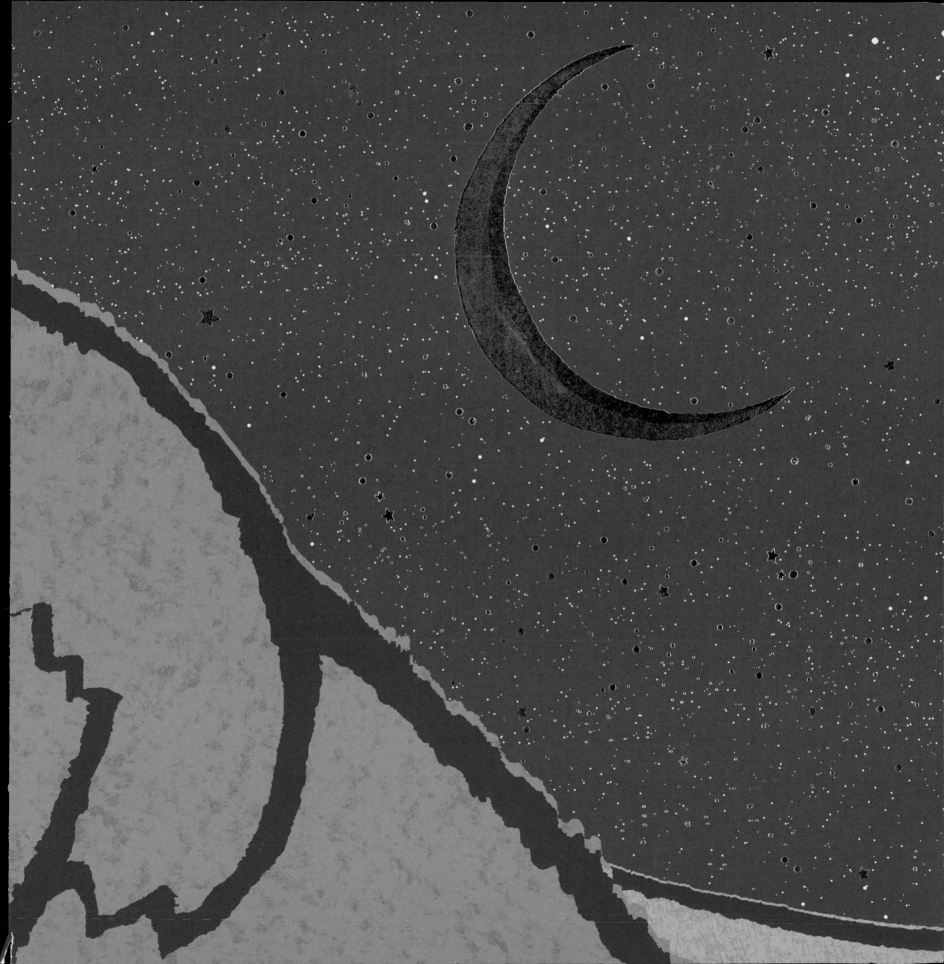

A TEMPLAR BOOK

First published in the UK in 2007 by Templar Publishing,
this softback edition published in 2013 by Templar Publishing,
an imprint of The Templar Company Limited,
Deepdene Lodge, Deepdene Avenue, Dorking, Surrey, RH5 4AT
www.templarco.co.uk

Copyright © 2007 by Emma Dodd

1 3 5 7 9 10 8 6 4 2

ISBN-13: 978-1-84877-825-2

Printed in China